LOUDMOUTH George
and the New Neighbors

LOUDMOUTH George
and the New Neighbors

Nancy Carlson

Carolrhoda Books, Inc. ♦ Minneapolis

LIBRARY OF CONGRESS CATALOGING IN PUBLICATION DATA

Carlson, Nancy L.
　　Loudmouth George and the new neighbors.

　　Summary: When a family of pigs moves in next door,
the rabbit George wants nothing to do with them, but
finally he gives in and finds out they aren't so bad
after all.
　　[1. Animals — Fiction. 2. Neighborliness — Fiction.
3. Prejudices — Fiction]
I. Title.
PZ7.C21665Lp　　1983　　　　　　[E]　　　　　　83-7298
ISBN 0-87614-216-1 (lib. bdg.)

　　2　3　4　5　6　7　8　9　10　92　91　90　89　88　87　86　85　84

for the Gals — Elaine, Tacy, and Beev

"Wake up, George," yelled his friend Harriet.
"You have new neighbors moving in next door!"

"It looks like they have kids our age," said Harriet.

"But, Harriet," said George, "they're PIGS!"

"So what?" said Harriet. "Let's go meet them."

"Are you crazy?" said George. "I don't want to meet any pigs!"

"Well, I do," said Harriet.

"But pigs are dirty," said George. "They eat garbage. They're not like us at all. I'm going to go play with Ralph."

"Suit yourself," said Harriet, "but I think you're being stupid."

"Can Ralph come out and play?" George
asked Ralph's mom.

"He's not at home, George," said Mrs. Duncan. "I think he might have gone to meet the new neighbors."

"This is getting disgusting," said George.

That day George played by himself.

On Tuesday morning George was in his backyard.

"Why don't you come over and play with
me?" Louanne Pig called across the fence.

"No thanks," said George.

"I'm not going to play with any smelly old pigs," he mumbled to himself.

On Wednesday George heard laughter outside. He looked out the window. There were Harriet and Ralph and Louanne running through the Pigs' sprinkler.

"I think I'll just stay inside today," said
George.

By lunchtime he couldn't stand it anymore. "They sure sound like they're having fun over there."

George strolled into his backyard.

"Come on over, George," said Harriet. "The water's great."

"Well," said George, "I'm kind of busy, but maybe just for a minute." He jumped over the fence.

George stayed all afternoon.

On Thursday the four of them played football.
On Friday they played with flying saucers.

On Saturday they were getting a game of croquet going when Ralph came tearing into Louanne's yard.

"Guess what?" he said. "There's a family of cats
moving in next door to me. Let's go meet them."

"Cats!" thought George. "Cats have claws. They spit and hiss. They're not like us at all."

"Aren't you coming, George?" said Harriet.

"Well," said George, "maybe just for a minute."

DATE			

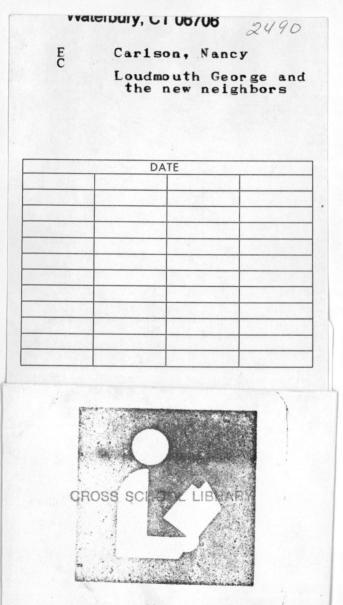